P9-CRZ-846

Into the Spotlight

DANVILLE PUBLIC LIBRARY
Danville, Indiana

by Erin Falligant

illustrated by Arcana Studios

⭐ American Girl®

Published by American Girl Publishing, Inc.
Copyright © 2011 by American Girl, LLC

All rights reserved. No part of this book may be used or reproduced
in any manner whatsoever without written permission except in the case
of brief quotations embodied in critical articles and reviews.

Questions or comments? Call 1-800-845-0005, visit our Web site at
americangirl.com, or write to Customer Service, American Girl,
8400 Fairway Place, Middleton, WI 53562-0497.

Printed in China
11 12 13 14 15 16 LEO 10 9 8 7 6 5 4 3 2 1

All American Girl and Innerstar University marks and Amber™, Emmy™,
Isabel™, Logan™, Neely™, Paige™, Riley™, and Shelby™ are trademarks
of American Girl, LLC.

This book is a work of fiction. Any similarity to real persons, living or dead,
is coincidental and not intended by American Girl. References to real events,
people, or places are used fictitiously. Other names, characters, places, and
incidents are the products of imagination.

Illustrated by Thu Thai at Arcana Studios

Special thanks to dancer Camille Wirkus and owner/instructor Shannon
Gallagher at Premier Dance Academy, LLC, Madison, Wisconsin

Cataloging-in-Publication Data available from the Library of Congress

INNERSTARU.com

Welcome to Innerstar University! At this imaginary, one-of-a-kind school, you can live with your friends in a dorm called Brightstar House and find lots of fun ways to let your true talents shine. Your friends at Innerstar U will help you find your way through some challenging situations, too.

When you reach a page in this book that asks you to make a decision, choose carefully. The decisions you make will lead to more than 20 different endings! (*Hint:* Use a pencil to check off your choices. That way, you'll never read the same story twice.)

Want to try another ending? Read the book again—and then again. Find out what would have happened if you'd made *different* choices. Then head to www.innerstarU.com for even more book endings, games, and fun with friends.

Innerstar Guides

Every girl needs a few good friends to help her find her way. These are the friends who are always there for **you**.

Emmy

A brave girl who loves swimming and boating

Isabel

A confident girl with a funky sense of style

Riley

A good sport, on the field and off

Paige

A nature lover who leads hikes and campus cleanups

Amber

An animal lover and
a loyal friend

Neely

A creative girl who loves
dance, music, and art

Logan

A super-smart girl
who is curious about
EVERYTHING

Shelby

A kind girl who is there
for her friends—and loves
making NEW friends!

Innerstar U Campus

1. Rising Star Stables
2. Star Student Center
3. Brightstar House
4. Starlight Library
5. Sparkle Studios
6. Blue Sky Nature Center

[Y]ou hurry down the dark aisle, hoping to find your seat before the curtains part and the next routine begins. U-Shine Hall is packed with students, all here to watch the spring dance recital. Every head looks the same from the back—until you spot Isabel's telltale curls. *Phew!*

"It's about time!" Isabel says as you slide into your seat beside her.

Riley, who is sitting on the other side of Isabel, leans forward to say hello. She taps her watch playfully and shakes her blonde head at you. "You almost missed it!" she says. "Neely's routine is next."

As the heavy berry-colored curtain slides open, you try to quiet your breathing. Your friend Neely has a solo part in this routine, and you promised her you'd be here for it. It looks as though you made it just in time.

 Turn to page 10.

The stage is dark. It takes your eyes a few seconds to make out the row of dancers standing in the shadows. Their bodies are poised, still as statues. When the music begins, they slowly come alive, one by one.

"There she is!" Isabel says, nudging you with her elbow. Sure enough, there's Neely. She's wearing a floaty pink ballet skirt and is standing on tiptoe.

You knew Neely was a good dancer, but you never knew *how* good. She flits like a butterfly across the stage.

When the music changes, the other dancers step back. The spotlight finds Neely, and she begins a graceful series of steps, leaps, and twirls. You hold your breath—partly out of nervousness and partly in wonder. You can't believe that's your friend up there, the same girl you studied with just yesterday.

In the bright spotlight, it's as if Neely is the only dancer onstage—the only person in the room. You can't take your eyes off her.

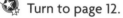 Turn to page 12.

After the recital, you, Isabel, and Riley work your way through the crowd to meet Neely near the changing rooms. Riley is carrying a bouquet of pink roses for Neely. You wish you'd thought of that.

"They can be from all of us," Riley says kindly.

You find Neely by the water fountain. She's still in her ballet skirt, her cheeks flushed and her eyes bright. When she sees the three of you, she rushes forward to gather you into a group hug.

"Thanks so much for coming!" Neely says. "It really means a lot to me."

"We wouldn't have missed it," says Isabel. "You were *amazing*."

"It's true," you add. "I wish I could dance like that."

"So do I," says Riley wistfully.

Neely cocks her head. "Well . . ." she says. "There *is* a beginning ballet class starting up next week. I'm going to help teach it. You guys should come!"

You and Riley look at each other. Riley's head is already bobbing up and down enthusiastically. She's always game for anything.

As for you, you're a little nervous about committing to something you've never tried. Plus, you're really busy— you and your friend Logan were just elected to the student council here at Innerstar University.

"What do you say?" Riley asks you.

"I don't know," you say. "Sounds great, but I have so much going on right now. Can I think about it?"

"Of course," says Neely. "But the class is filling up fast." She points to a sign-up sheet on the bulletin board hanging over the fountain. There are only a few empty lines under a long list of signatures.

"You guys should do it!" says Isabel. "I'd join, too, if I wasn't already taking tap."

You're feeling the pressure now. All eyes are on you. What do you do?

 If you say yes, turn to page 14.

If you decide to sit in on a class before making up your mind, turn to page 16.

If you say no because you're too busy, turn to page 17.

"Let's do it," you say to Riley. She lets loose a cheer and grabs the pen hanging by the sign-up sheet.

As soon as you sign up for ballet class, butterflies of excitement start dancing in your stomach. Now that you've committed, you can't wait to get started!

"I'm going to need something to wear to class," you think out loud.

Isabel is already two steps ahead of you. "I know where you can find cute leotards," she says. And before you know it, you're on your way to the Shopping Square, with red-headed Isabel leading the way.

As you step through the door of Bravo Boutique, you scan the store for pink leotards. But Isabel has other ideas.

"How about this?" she asks, holding up a zebra-print leotard.

You're speechless. You breathe a sigh of relief when you see a rack full of other dancewear behind Isabel. "I was thinking about something more, um, basic," you say, pointing to the rack.

Isabel shrugs and slides the striped leotard back onto the rack. She's so brave—she's always experimenting with new looks. But you want to look like a classical ballerina, just like Neely did as she danced across that stage.

 Turn to page 18.

It's hard not to say yes—especially with Riley staring at you, holding her breath—but you're not ready to commit to something you don't know anything about.

"You go ahead and sign up," you say to Riley. "I think I need to watch a class before I decide."

Riley's okay with that, as long as you promise to go with her to the first class. And so you do. As class begins, you find a chair just inside the door of the studio.

Neely and the instructor help the beginning dancers do some stretching and then go through some basic positions for feet and arms. Riley seems to be having fun. She keeps turning around to make sure you're still watching. You grin and give her a thumbs-up.

By the time class is halfway over, though, you're pretty sure ballet class isn't for you. It's nothing like watching a ballet performance. It looks as if there's a whole lot to learn before a dancer can hit the stage.

After class, you wait in the hall while Riley changes her clothes. You run into Isabel, who's just arriving for her tap dance lessons. "What'd you think of ballet class?" she asks.

You shrug. "I don't think it's for me," you say.

Isabel nods. "That's okay," she says. "At least now you know." She starts to walk away but then says, "Do you want to watch some tap, since you're already here?"

 Turn to page 35.

The more you think about it, the more you realize you probably shouldn't sign up for ballet class. You have to be realistic about how many things you can pack into a week.

"Sorry, guys," you say. "I'm just too busy."

You know you made the right decision as soon as you leave U-Shine Hall. Logan is running toward you with a flyer, a reminder of tonight's student council meeting. You're getting together to brainstorm ideas for Innerstar U's annual fund-raiser.

"Can you come?" Logan asks hopefully. She was just elected student council president, which is a big deal for her. You promise her that you'll be there.

At the meeting, you can tell Logan is really nervous, so you try to be extra supportive of her and her ideas. When she suggests a bake sale for the fund-raiser, you tell her it's a great idea—even though you were hoping to do something more original. In fact, spending the afternoon at U-Shine Hall gave you a super-fun fund-raising idea: a dance-a-thon!

 If you stay quiet to support Logan and her idea, turn to page 20.

 If you share your idea, turn to page 19.

As soon as you get back to your room at Brightstar House, you dump everything out of your shopping bag onto your bed.

"Try it on!" says Isabel, who won't leave until she sees you modeling your new gear.

The tights are a little hard to get into, but the leotard slips right on and is super comfortable. Then you step into your ballet shoes. Your stomach sinks when you see that the elastic straps aren't attached to the slippers. You have to sew them on, and you don't know how to sew.

"I can help you with that," says Isabel. She runs back to her room and returns a few minutes later with a mini sewing kit. While she stitches the straps carefully to the insides of your shoes, you check out the rest of your outfit in your full-length mirror.

Wow—you look like a dancer already! You stand on tiptoe and do a twirl. You can't dance like Neely yet, but you're determined to give it all you've got until you can.

 Turn to page 22.

You give everyone a little time to talk about the bake sale. Then you raise your hand and say, "A bake sale is a great idea. I have another idea, too. How about a dance-a-thon?"

"What's that?" someone asks curiously.

"It's kind of like a 'dance 'til you drop' contest," you explain. "We could invite our classmates to buy tickets to come or to enter the contest, and we could raise extra money by selling concessions and raffle tickets."

You're relieved to see Logan's eyes light up at your suggestion. "Yes!" she says. "That's it!" The other council members agree.

You start planning the dance-a-thon right away. You look for a DJ who'll play the kind of music you and your friends love. You and Logan go together to the Star Student Center to see if you can reserve a large hall there for the dance. Then you print out sign-up sheets for dance teams. You post them in the cafeteria and in the hallway at U-Shine Hall.

Turn to page 23.

You can see how passionate Logan is about the bake sale, so you support her idea. You help Logan bake twelve batches of cookies, brownies, and muffins. Whew! The day of the sale, you arrange the treats on tables in front of the Star Student Center.

It's windy out, which makes it really hard to keep the napkins and paper plates from flying away. When it starts to sprinkle, you hold a newspaper over the treats and smile at Logan, trying to keep her spirits up. Then the clouds open and it starts to pour.

Now you have no choice—you have to move everything inside. You race back and forth carrying boxes of cupcakes and bags of cookies. You finish out the sale of a few soggy brownies just inside the doors of the student center, while the rain comes down in sheets outside.

Logan is really discouraged, especially when you count the money at the end of the sale. You didn't raise nearly as much as you thought you would.

Turn to page 26.

The day of your first ballet lesson, you and Riley hurry down the path from Brightstar House to U-Shine Hall. You're dressed in your new pink leotard, and you have your ballet slippers tucked safely in your duffle bag.

When you step into the dance studio, you stand still for a moment to take it all in. The wooden floor gleams, and the mirrored walls seem to stretch on and on. There are lots of dancers in the room, and they all look as nervous as you feel—except for Neely, junior instructor, who greets you and Riley at the door with a huge smile.

You've just stepped into your ballet slippers when the lead instructor claps her hands to call the class to attention. She explains that classes normally start at the *barre,* the wooden rail that runs along the mirrored walls. Because you are beginners, you'll start with exercises on the floor instead. You suddenly feel nervous.

 If you sit behind Riley so that you can hide a little, turn to page 24.

 If you sit in the front row so that you can see the instructor better, turn to page 27.

You check the sign-up sheets throughout the week. By Friday, three dance teams have signed up to compete in the dance-a-thon.

Neely is captain of one of the teams, and lots of her dancer friends signed up with her. A girl named Devin is captain of the second team. And the last team? That one's yours. You decided to show your support for the fundraiser by leading a team made up of your own friends.

Rivalry among the teams is already in full force. It's friendly competition, of course—at least between your team and Neely's. Devin, on the other hand, is taking things pretty seriously. She has a reputation for being super competitive.

You figure that Devin's competitive streak could be a good thing, though. The more that she talks up the contest, the more people will turn out to see it!

Turn to page 28.

You sit with your legs stretched outward in a V shape. The instructor asks you to lean forward, stretching first toward the center and then over each leg. You stretch again with your legs together, straight out in front of you. You finish by putting the soles of your feet together and leaning forward.

The stretching exercises aren't hard, but your muscles feel stiff and tight. You're a little embarrassed to see how flexible Riley is compared to you. She can almost touch her forehead to the floor!

Must be from all that yoga she does, you think.

After stretching, you stand up, and the instructor talks about the five basic positions for your feet and arms. You stand in first position with your heels together and your toes pointed outward. It's a little tough for you. You can't turn your feet out very far. Third and fourth positions are even harder because you have to cross your feet, one in front of the other.

Neely comes over to check your position. "Don't force it," she says. "It'll get easier, with practice."

But as you practice the positions again—this time at the barre, in front of the mirror—you sneak a peek at Riley. She's standing behind you, her feet turned out perfectly.

 Turn to page 30.

"Maybe we should have thought up a different project," Logan says sadly as you walk back to Brightstar House.

"I was wondering about that, too," you say. "Maybe next time we could try a dance-a-thon."

Logan stops walking and looks at you. "That's a great idea," she says. "Why didn't you mention it at the meeting?"

You shrug. "I didn't want to disagree with your bake-sale idea," you say. "You seemed so excited about it."

Logan's jaw drops. "It's okay to disagree," she says. "You have great ideas! A real leader speaks her mind and *shares* her ideas. That's what you were elected for, right?"

You're embarrassed now. You kind of blew your chance to help raise good money for the school. Next time, you'll open your mouth and let those great ideas flow.

The End

A real leader speaks her mind and shares her ideas.

You take a spot on the floor in front of the instructor, who leads you through some stretching exercises. The backs of your legs feel tight, so you ease into the stretches, trying not to force them.

After stretching, you stand up to learn the five basic positions for your feet and arms. Neely and the instructor demonstrate first position, with their heels together and their toes pointed outward. Neely rounds her arms and raises them out in front of her. She looks so elegant. You're excited to try the position.

You put your heels together, but your toes don't want to turn outward. The more you try, the more wobbly you feel. You step your feet apart for second position, which feels a little easier. You separate your arms, too, and try to stand tall and steady.

As you move through the next three positions, you watch yourself in the mirror. You can't help noticing that your body looks kind of clumsy and awkward. You may be dressed like a ballerina, but you're not nearly as graceful as one.

You sigh. This is going to take some work.

 Turn to page 31.

The day of the dance-a-thon, students stream into the student center. The dance floor is already full, and Logan is hard at work selling raffle tickets and *shout-outs*— messages you can pay the DJ to deliver to your friends over the sound system.

You empty your pockets and find a few crumpled bills and loose change. It all adds up to about five dollars— enough for five shout-outs or one raffle ticket.

The raffle prizes are pretty cool: a kite from the Bright Kites tent, a gift certificate to Bravo Boutique, and dance classes from U-Shine Hall. Still, the shout-outs would be fun. Your friends would be so surprised!

What do you spend your money on?

 If you buy shout-outs, turn to page 32.

If you buy a raffle ticket, turn to page 34.

Your favorite part of class is when the instructor calls you away from the barre to do some jumps and leaps. Well, you're not really leaping. You start out by skipping, which is good practice for leaping. But it feels good to finally be moving.

"Point your toes," the instructor reminds you and your classmates. "Step in time with the music."

You try to focus on her words, but as you skip across the floor, your mind wanders. You flash back to Neely's performance, except this time, you imagine that you're right up there on stage with her. You're wearing your own pink tutu, and you're leaping through the air as if you have wings.

When you snap back to attention, you find yourself skipping so fast and so high that you suddenly lose your footing. You come down hard and barrel right into the dancer in front of you, who lurches forward and lands sprawled on the wooden floor.

"Easy now!" the instructor scolds. "Stay in control of your body."

"Um, sorry," you mumble, offering a hand to the dancer on the floor. You feel your face flush crimson, something you *can't* control. Neely flashes you a sympathetic smile.

 Turn to page 33.

When your instructor invites you and your classmates to practice some jumps, you feel a rush of excitement. This should be fun!

You stand in second position and try a *sauté*, jumping straight up in the air and then landing in the same position you started from. You jump again. You bend your knees, push against the floor, and spring into the air. As you jump again and again, you watch yourself in the mirror, thinking, *Hey, I don't look half bad!*

Your instructor stops in front of you and smiles. You're sure she's going to compliment you on your vertical leap, but instead she says, "Listen to the music, now. You guys aren't popcorn. You need to land at the same time." She snaps her fingers, helping you find the rhythm.

Popcorn? Great. So far, not so good.

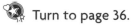 Turn to page 36.

You settle on the shout-outs. You can't wait to see your friends' faces when the DJ delivers your messages!

You see Isabel, Riley, Logan, and a few other teammates on the dance floor. You work your way through the crowd to join them. By the time the official dance contest starts, you're having so much fun that you've nearly forgotten about the shout-outs—until the first one rings out over the sound system.

You're dancing with Logan, doing some silly shoulder moves, when the DJ says, "This shout-out goes to Logan, who's a great leader on and off the dance floor. Girl, you rule!"

Logan freezes, her green eyes wide. Then she bursts into laughter. "Who did that?!" she asks, glancing around your circle of friends.

You can't look Logan in the eye—or stop laughing—so she busts you. But after that, she seems to be having more fun than ever, and she *does* become a leader on the dance floor. Her shoulder moves turn into full-body moves. She starts really getting into it, and pretty soon everyone on your team is copying her.

 Turn to page 39.

Class ends with a *reverence*, a curtsy that the dancers do to say good-bye and thank you to the instructor. You're wondering if maybe you should say good-bye to ballet class altogether. You're still embarrassed about crashing into another dancer. Your pride is hurt, too, by how much easier dancing seems to come to Riley than it does to you.

As you leave the classroom, you wonder if you should ask Neely for some private lessons. She's talking with the instructor at the back of the room. You're about to approach Neely when Riley runs up from behind you and throws her arm around your shoulders.

"Wasn't that great?" she asks.

You hesitate. "It was a little hard for me, actually," you admit. "I'm not as flexible as you are."

"Oh," says Riley. She gives your shoulders another squeeze. "You should start coming to yoga with me," she says. "It's a great way to stretch your dancing muscles."

You've never tried yoga before. It obviously works for Riley, but will it work for you, too? And is yoga more important than getting extra dance help from Neely? You know you won't have time to do both.

If you say yes to yoga with Riley, turn to page 42.

If you tell her you're hoping to get extra dance lessons from Neely instead, turn to page 43.

You decide to buy a raffle ticket. You have your eye on that kite.

You stuff the ticket in your pocket and then search the dance floor for your team. Riley waves at you from across the room, and you wind your way through dancers to reach her. She, Isabel, Logan, and your other friends are dancing in a big circle. As you fall in beside them, you suddenly feel self-conscious.

Riley and Emmy are great dancers, maybe because they're so athletic. Isabel has fun, funky moves. Chances are, she's making most of them up, but she's so confident that she pulls them off. Shelby dances pretty well, too, probably because she's hosted her share of parties. Even Logan and Amber look comfortable on the dance floor.

You know a few dance moves, but when those run dry, you start looking around for inspiration. You glance over your shoulder and see Devin leading her team in a dance routine. It looks vaguely familiar. Maybe it's from the latest Strawberries music video?

You try to follow along, copying Devin's steps. She catches you studying her, and she gives you a smug smile. *I must look pretty clumsy,* you think. Good thing there aren't any mirrors in here. Sometimes it's better *not* to know what you look like!

 Turn to page 44.

You agree to watch Isabel's tap class. What do you have to lose?

As soon as class begins, you realize how different tap is from ballet. You love the sound of the shoes clapping and shuffling across the floor.

Isabel is really good. You admire her quick legs and feet. When the instructor asks her to demonstrate a few steps, she smiles confidently and walks to the middle of the floor.

"One and two and three and four . . ." the instructor counts, and Isabel's feet tap right in time. She holds her arms out and her head high. She looks like the star of one of those old black-and-white movies.

As impressed as you are with Isabel's dancing, you can't imagine yourself doing what she's doing. Isabel looks so natural on the dance floor. You don't think you could ever move so smoothly and confidently. By the end of the class, you've made a firm decision: you're not going to be a dancer. You're going to stick with student council instead.

 Turn to page 38.

At the end of class, the instructor invites Neely to demonstrate a few moves. Your stomach flutters, remembering Neely's amazing performance during the recital.

Neely does a few steps from her routine. She leaps, sways, and turns as if in time to some beautiful music that you can't hear. It turns out that she doesn't need a spotlight or a fancy tutu in order to shine. She's every bit as beautiful here in the classroom as she was onstage a week ago.

That's what I want to look like, you remind yourself. But after today's class, you know that you're going to have to work extra hard to get there.

 If you ask Neely for extra help, turn to page 43.

 If you ask Riley if she wants to practice together, turn to page 60.

You say good-bye to Isabel and then wind your way back to the main door of U-Shine Hall. You're glad to have finally made up your mind about dance. But then you spot something that stops you in your tracks.

Through the open door of a classroom, you see a girl spinning wildly across the floor. She's barefoot, dressed in a tank top and black tights cut off above the knees. She crouches low like a cat, ready to pounce. Then she springs into the air and releases her legs into a high kick. You can almost feel her energy coursing through your own body. The hair on your arms stands on end.

When the girl sees you standing in the doorway, she stops dancing and walks over to greet you. She doesn't seem at all embarrassed to have an audience.

"Wow," you say. It's all you can come up with.

"Do you like modern dance?" the girl asks, wiping the sweat from her forehead with a towel.

You shrug. You're still having trouble finding words. The truth is, you don't know a thing about modern dance. But after watching this girl dance, you definitely want to know more.

Turn to page 88.

Your next shout-out happens an hour into the dance-a-thon. Your feet are starting to hurt, and you can see that your friends are wearing down, too. Emmy, who had an all-day swim meet before the dance-a-thon, is really dragging.

Then the DJ gets on the microphone and delivers your message, just in time: "This shout-out goes to Emmy, who's as graceful in the pool as she is on the dance floor. Emmy, do the Swim!"

Emmy's head jerks upright, and she stares straight at you, a smile spreading quickly across her face. "*You* did that!" she says, pointing a finger. Then she grabs her nose with one hand, waves her other hand in the air as if through water, and does "the Swim." Other girls do it, too, and pretty soon your dance-a-thon turns into an energetic "swim-a-thon."

You love how your shout-outs have perked up your friends. You decide to look for other ways to make your friends laugh and keep the energy flowing.

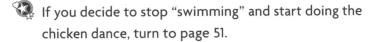

 If you decide to stop "swimming" and start doing the chicken dance, turn to page 51.

If you decide to make a real splash with a crazy dance of your own, turn to page 40.

"Hey, guys, try this!" you say to your friends.

You make up, right there on the spot, a "shout-out dance." You cup your mouth with your hand and shout "Hey!" Then you point dramatically at Logan and say, "You!" Then you cup your mouth with your other hand and point at Riley. You put one hand on your hip, twirl your other hand in the air, and hop around in a circle until you're facing Emmy and Isabel. Then you start the dance all over again.

Pretty soon all of your friends are doing the shout-out dance. They chant, "Hey . . . you!" "Hey . . . you!"

You see out of the corner of your eye that Devin is sneering at you. She obviously thinks your dance is pretty dumb, but then some of *her* teammates start doing it, too. Devin watches them for a moment, a disgusted look on her face. But the next time you glance over, she's doing the dance, too. In fact, everyone on the dance floor starts doing the shout-out dance. You can't believe what you've started!

 Turn to page 54.

You agree to go to yoga with Riley, even though a part of you is worried about trying yet *another* new thing.

The Real Spirit Center at Innerstar U is beautiful. The yoga instructor is leading an outdoor class today on the deck overlooking the heart-shaped pond. You unroll your mat and take a few deep breaths, reaching upward toward the sky. But about fifteen minutes into class, you're already completely frustrated. You watch Riley bend deeply and put her palms on the deck while you can barely touch your toes.

Riley glances over and sees the expression on your face. "It takes time," she whispers to you. "The more often you stretch, the more flexible you'll get."

As you leave class, you make a silent vow that you're going to spend every extra minute you have stretching. You do your homework while sitting on the floor of your room, the soles of your feet pressed together. You do the Tree Pose you learned in yoga while you wait in line for dinner at the cafeteria. You do spine twists during your student council meeting.

Sure, you get odd looks, but you tell yourself that it'll all be worth it. Pretty soon, you'll be as flexible as Riley. You'll be a better dancer then, too.

 Turn to page 45.

Neely agrees to give you extra help a couple of times a week, which is *great* news. You're sure that with Neely's tutoring, you're going to pick up ballet much more quickly.

You start early the next day. You meet Neely in the studio, and she walks you through the five positions—first in the center of the floor and then at the barre. Stretching and barre work take up most of the half hour you have together.

"Can you teach me anything else?" you ask her as you watch the clock. "Maybe a leap or one of those cool spins you do?"

Neely laughs. "You're not quite ready for those yet," she says, "but keep practicing, and you'll get there."

Turn to page 49.

You're amazed at how tired you are after just a few songs. After an hour, your feet are killing you. After two hours, you can't feel your feet at all.

Your energetic dancing has become little more than stepping from side to side. You clap your hands now and then and maybe spin in a circle, but only when Devin looks your way. You don't want her to think your team is giving up anytime soon.

The problem is, you're afraid your team *will* give up soon. Your teammates are really dragging. The rules say that only one dancer can sit out at a time. You and your friends take turns resting, but never for long enough.

 If you think it's time to quit, turn to page 46.

 If you think you can re-energize your friends, turn to page 50.

You head to your next ballet class feeling great, except for the sharp pain on the inside of your left leg. You might have overdone it a bit in the stretching department. You limp into U-Shine Hall, where the other dancers are already stretching on the floor.

Today, your instructor leads you through the five basic positions again. This time, though, she has you do *demi-pliés*, or half knee bends. You turn out your feet, heels together.

As you bend your knees and lower yourself into the plié, pain sears through your inner thigh. You gasp and hop away from the barre.

"What is it?" Neely asks, running over to steady you.

"I think I . . . *ouch*," is all you can say.

By now, the instructor is beside you, too, helping you lower yourself to the floor. She quickly figures out that you pulled a muscle. You have to sit out the rest of class and explain to your instructor—and Neely and Riley—how you hurt yourself.

Riley keeps apologizing to you, as if this is her fault. "I'm sorry," she says again. "Didn't I mention that getting more flexible takes time?"

You nod sadly. "You did," you reassure her. "I just wasn't very patient."

 Turn to page 48.

Finally, it's official: Emmy is wrecked, she's so tired. Isabel wore the wrong shoes, and she winces every time she moves. Even Riley, who's usually so full of energy, looks as if she could fall asleep standing up. Your team votes to quit, and the truth is, you're relieved that it's all over.

You stay to cheer on Neely's team to victory. After Devin's team packs it in, Neely's eyes are still bright, and she looks as if she could keep dancing all night. If you had to lose to someone, you're glad it's your good friend— who's also a great dancer.

You're standing beside Neely when the DJ calls out the results of the raffle drawing. "I'm hoping for the kite," you whisper to Neely. You cross your fingers and grin at her.

"No way," she says. "You're so winning the dance lessons." She winks at you.

You don't win the kite or the dance lessons, but that's okay. You don't think you'll have the urge to dance again anytime soon.

The good news is that the dance-a-thon raised a *lot* of money for Innerstar U. You may not be an award-winning dancer, but you do have some good ideas!

The End

Your instructor says that a pulled muscle can take a couple of weeks to heal. She suggests that you drop out of this ballet class and wait for the next one to start.

Neely sees the shocked look on your face. "It's okay," she reassures you. "We start a new class every few months. I promise to save a spot for you in the next one."

You're devastated, but you know that all of this is your own fault. You spent so much time comparing yourself to Riley that you lost sight of what you were supposed to be doing and learning.

Neely sits with you for a while after class. She reminds you that dancing is about taking care of your body, not hurting it. "And remember," she scolds gently, "the only person you should be focusing on in class is *yourself*."

Thanks to your injury, you'll have plenty of time to do just that while you wait for the *next* class to start.

The End

You practice ballet four times a week—twice in class and twice with Neely. After a couple of weeks, you feel more flexible, but you're still practicing the same things over and over again: first position, second position, pliés, relevés . . .

You and Neely are standing side by side at the barre, practicing grand pliés, when you decide that you can't take it anymore. It's time to ask Neely straight-out when you'll be able to learn something new. "When can I move on from these positions and start dancing the way you do?" you ask Neely. You carefully watch her expression in the mirror.

Neely gives you a confused look. "Move on?" she says. "I've been dancing for six years, and I *still* start each and every practice with these positions."

Oh. Your stomach sinks. It suddenly dawns on you that it's going to take more than a few weeks to start dancing like Neely does. It may take months or even years. It may never happen at all.

 If you tell Neely how frustrated you feel, turn to page 52.

 If you keep quiet, turn to page 59.

You've got to do something to perk up your friends, but what? You glance at Isabel, who you know has been taking tap dance lessons.

"Hey, Isabel," you say, "can you teach me a tap step?"

Isabel straightens up and smiles. "Definitely!" she says. "Let's see now . . ." She stops for a moment to think, and then she says, "Okay, here's one. This is called the 'shuffle hop step.'" She slides her right foot forward and backward, hops on her left foot, and then steps onto her right. She switches feet and does it again. It looks like fun!

The rest of you try the shuffle hop step, with a few more pointers from Isabel. Learning tap takes your mind off your sore feet. One look at your friends' faces tells you that they're all getting their second wind, too.

Neely catches sight of your mini tap routine, and she and the dancers on her team start doing some tap. They're all such great dancers. You bet they know a ton of moves they could teach you.

 If you ask Neely's team to teach your team some moves, turn to page 53.

 If you focus on your own team and ask if any of your friends wants to teach a step, turn to page 57.

"It's time for the chicken dance!" you announce, squawking like a bird. You open and close your hands like little bird beaks, and then you tuck your hands into your armpits and flap your elbows like chicken wings. You twist your body a few times and finish with some claps.

Everyone on your team cracks up, and then they start flapping their own wings. After that, Shelby gets everyone doing the Twist. She gets down so low to the ground that you're sure she's going to fall over, but she doesn't. She's really good!

Isabel shows you her best disco moves, straight out of the seventies. Logan does something she calls the Robot. Then Riley teaches the team how to do some basic hip-hop. You're pretty sure that your hip-hop moves don't look anything like Riley's, but you're having so much fun now that you don't even care.

Before you know it, two more hours have gone by, and you and your friends are still going strong!

 Turn to page 56.

You take a deep breath and then tell Neely exactly how you feel. "I'm working hard," you say. "I really am. But I'm just not getting anywhere."

Neely smiles. "I get it," she says. "Ballet is a *ton* of work, and it takes time. But if you really love it and stick with it, all your work will be worth it."

You picture Neely dancing onstage, and you know that she's right—her work has paid off. You're just not sure *you* love ballet enough to stick with it for that long.

Neely studies your face. She must be able to tell now that you're having serious doubts about ballet. "I hope you'll stay in class at least until the first performance," she says. "But why don't you sleep on it, and we can talk more tomorrow?"

You agree to meet Neely back in the studio tomorrow. You trudge back to your room at Brightstar House, your head spinning with indecision. By the time you go to bed, you still don't know what you're going to do about ballet class. But when the sun streams through your window the next morning, things seem much clearer.

If you decide to stay in class, turn to page 65.

If you decide to quit, turn to page 61.

You ask Neely if she and her teammates can show your team a few cool dance moves. It feels weird to ask, because you guys are supposed to be competing. But you remind yourself that anything that keeps both groups dancing will be a good thing for the fund-raiser. And it'll be more fun that way, too.

Neely's teammates share a couple of jazz and tap steps. Time passes quickly while you're learning, and you're surprised to glance up at the clock and see that not only has another hour and a half gone by, but that Devin's team is packing it in. One of her friends is limping out the door, carrying her shoes in her hands.

When it's time for the DJ to pack it up, your team and Neely's are *still* having fun with your dance "lessons." You declare a tie between the teams, and that feels really good.

As you walk out the door with Neely, you declare something else: that maybe you *do* want to take some dance lessons at U-Shine Hall. After all, you already have one lesson—one really l-o-n-g lesson—under your belt!

The End

Now there's no stopping you. New dance moves are springing out of your fingers, your arms, your legs, and your hips. Your energy and creativity must be contagious, because your friends are making up new moves, too.

All of the dance teams are going strong. You see that Neely's team is doing some cross between ballet and hip-hop. Everyone is laughing and having fun.

You take a few quick breaks to get something to drink and to rest your feet. When you check your watch, you're amazed to see that four hours have gone by. Your body feels like a limp noodle, but you're still grinning from ear to ear.

Your team wins second place in the dance-a-thon, right after Neely's team of hip-hop ballerinas. You had a great time, and you inspired your friends. In fact, you inspired *all* of the dancers. Because they were having so much fun and danced for so long, they bought more concessions, raffle tickets, and shout-outs than you and Logan expected them to. The fund-raiser was a huge success!

Turn to page 58.

You're having so much fun with your friends, you barely notice that Neely's team has quit dancing. Most of the girls are sitting down, rubbing their feet—but not Neely. She's on her way over to support your team and cheer you on.

Devin's team drops out, too. You can tell by the scowl on Devin's face that she's disappointed in her team. *Maybe she should have taught them the chicken dance,* you think to yourself. It sure kept your team going!

You gladly accept the "Dance 'til You Drop" award for your team, and you're rewarded again when you help Logan count the money from the night's event. You earned more than eleven hundred dollars for Innerstar U!

You feel like a real leader, a girl with great ideas and the courage to share them with others. You love student council, but after tonight, you know that you love dancing with your friends, too. Hmm . . . Maybe it's time to revisit those dance lessons at U-Shine Hall?

The End

DANCE 'TIL YOU DROP

You remind yourself to quit focusing on Neely's team and to take better care of your own. "Who's next?" you ask, inviting your friends to teach one another what they know.

Paige raises her hand enthusiastically. She wants to lead a line dance. You line up in two rows and follow her steps and spins. The DJ sees you line dancing and starts playing a popular country song, which makes you all laugh—and makes the dance a whole lot easier!

After that, you form a circle and play a dancing version of Follow the Leader. Any girl who wants to lead can jump in the middle and show a new move. It's hilarious—and fun.

Some of your friends love to lead. Isabel and Riley are in the middle *all* the time. Other girls, like Logan and Amber, hang back in the circle. They're having more fun watching their friends dance and following along. What about you?

 If you take your turn and dance in the middle of the circle, turn to page 64.

 If you hang back and let your friends do the leading, turn to page 66.

Logan announces the winners of the raffle, and then she says she has one more shout-out. "This one goes to you," she says.

When you look up, you see Logan pointing right at YOU. "Here's to the girl who thought up the dance-a-thon and who kept us all going tonight!" she says. Everyone claps, and you curtsy, your face hot with pride.

Then Neely taps you on the shoulder. She says she might need a little help teaching the next round of dance lessons. "Are you interested?" she asks, smiling playfully.

You're shocked. "Me?" you say. "But I've never even *taken* dance lessons!"

"You could be our inspiration," Neely says. "The person who motivates us and keeps things fun."

You're not sure if Neely's offer is serious, but you appreciate it just the same. "I'll think about it," you say. "Thanks!"

Your head is spinning from all of the excitement, and your feet are suddenly starting to throb. You can't wait to be back in your room at Brightstar House, climbing into your bed. It's definitely time to take off your dancing shoes—at least for now.

The End

You can't tell Neely how you really feel, not after she has spent so much time tutoring you. You continue with ballet, and your frustration builds. Instead of getting easier, lessons seem to get more difficult again.

Neely tries to be encouraging. She calls you her "star student," but you feel clumsy and awkward compared to her—and even compared to Riley. While you struggle at the barre, you watch Riley breeze through ballet moves. She's a natural, and it's pretty clear to you that you're *not*.

You're shocked, then, when Riley announces to you and Neely after class one day that she has decided to quit ballet.

"I'm just too busy with other sports," Riley says sadly. "I like ballet, but I guess I'm more of a team-sport kind of girl."

 Turn to page 70.

Practicing with Riley is so much fun! You work together in your room, checking your posture in the little mirror over your vanity. Sometimes you clear space for dancing in your walk-in closet, where you have a full-length mirror.

Only one of you can see herself in the mirror at a time, but that's okay. You prefer it when Riley is your "mirror." She gives you tips for improvement, but she gives you a lot of compliments, too. That makes you feel better about your progress.

You encourage Riley, too. She's a good dancer, so she doesn't always need pointers for how to do things better. Instead, you tell her about all the things you think she's doing well.

"Thanks," Riley says. "You're such a great teammate. I always feel better when I have my friends around me, helping me do my best."

You never thought of dancing as a team sport before, but Riley's words give you an idea. You look at the photos of your friends taped up around your vanity mirror. When you mention your idea to Riley, her eyes light up.

"Let's do it!" she says.

 Turn to page 62.

You walk to U-Shine Hall with determined steps, ready to tell Neely that ballet is just not for you. The door to the dance studio is closed, and when you peek through the window, you see that Neely is inside taking a lesson.

You lean against the door and watch for a while. The students in the classroom today look much more advanced than you are. You recognize one or two of them from the spring recital.

The dancers are doing *grand jetés,* great leaps through the air, from one corner of the classroom to the other. You know that jumps and leaps are usually the last part of the lesson, so Neely's class will be over soon.

 If you wait just outside the classroom for her, turn to page 69.

If you explore U-Shine Hall while you wait, turn to page 75.

That night at dinner, you and Riley ask Isabel if she wants to practice dance with you. Isabel is a tap dancer, but that doesn't mean she can't join your "team."

You teach Isabel the five basic positions of ballet. It's funny how much more interesting they seem when you're teaching them to someone else. You also realize how much easier they feel after a few weeks of practicing.

Isabel, in turn, shares some of her tap steps with you and Riley. Sometimes you get creative and combine steps so that you're doing "tap ballet" or "ballet tap." You laugh, wondering what Neely would think if she saw you. There's nothing graceful about those made-up moves, but they sure are fun!

When your friend Shelby joins your team, too, things get really interesting. Shelby used to take jazz lessons, so she has a few moves of her own to share. Shelby leads you in a sideways jazz walk across her bedroom floor. Then she teaches you the jazz step turn. She steps and pivots in a tight little circle, her arms raised at her sides and her hands perfectly poised.

Shelby walks you through the steps: "Left foot, pivot, right foot, pivot, left foot around, and—oh!" Shelby's leg hooks yours, and you both hit the floor. You lie there in a tangled pile of limbs, laughing hysterically. *Dancing is the best team sport ever,* you think to yourself as you help Shelby up so that you can try it all again.

 Turn to page 67.

It's a little scary to step out of the safety of the circle and head to the middle, but as soon as you do, your friends start cheering you on. You don't even think about what move you're going to show. You just let your body decide for you.

The next thing you know, you're doing some version of the bicycle dance. You're lifting up your knees—the right and then the left—and lunging them behind your body, as if pedaling a bike backward. You're having so much fun that Riley has to practically bump you out of the middle so that she can share a move of her own.

Your team has more energy now than they did when the night began. *We could do this all night!* you think to yourself. And you almost do. Devin's team drops out. Neely's team follows soon after, and they come to watch your team dance.

By the end of the night, you realize that you love learning new moves. You also like making up your own. If this student council thing doesn't pan out, you might have a future in dance—or at least a spot in a dance studio near you!

The End

You choose to stick with ballet, at least until the first performance. You'll dance as a shooting star in a silver satin costume. Your part in the show is small, but you decide to do the best you can with it. You work hard over the next couple of weeks to polish your "star jumps."

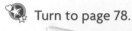 Turn to page 78.

You decide to let your friends lead the dances tonight. You're just having so much fun watching them! Everyone dances for another hour and a half. Your team doesn't win the dance-a-thon, but it comes in second—right after Neely's team.

By the end of the night, you've learned some great new moves from your friends. You've also learned something else: you may never be the world's greatest dancer, but you do know how to organize events and energize your friends—and *those* are talents, too.

The End

All that practice and fun with your friends pays off in the dance studio. You're remembering the positions and steps and are definitely getting more flexible. Neely notices that during barre work. "You look great!" she says as you lift your leg up behind you in an *arabesque*.

You feel pretty great, too. The problem comes when you step away from the barre and can see your form in the mirror. You're so used to practicing in your room, away from mirrors. When you can actually see your reflection, you realize that you don't *look* nearly as elegant as you feel.

You try focusing your eyes on the floor in front of you, but it's hard to hold your balance that way. Your instructor keeps telling you to lift your chin, but whenever you do, you find something else in the mirror to criticize.

Your negative thoughts are really starting to get you down. How can you stop being so hard on yourself?

 If you tell your friends how you're feeling and ask them for help, turn to page 74.

 If you're too embarrassed to talk about it with your friends, turn to page 68.

You try to quiet the little voice in your head, but every time you get in the dance studio, it starts back up again: *Lift your leg higher. Pull your stomach in tighter.* You just don't think you're measuring up.

When Neely announces that your class will perform a routine in the next recital, your stomach drops. You can't imagine getting in front of an audience when you still look like such a beginner.

Riley, of course, is thrilled about the performance. "Can you believe it?" she says happily as you walk back to Brightstar House. "You and me. Up on the stage. In the spotlight. In front of a huge crowd of people!"

Ack! you think, mentally plugging your ears. You take a deep breath, trying to keep your heart from racing. You can't stop picturing that audience. What if *they* see you the way that *you* see yourself when you look in the mirror?

Turn to page 71.

You can't seem to tear yourself away from the classroom window. The dancers are so strong and elegant. Neely is the most elegant of them all. When she finishes class, you tell her so. You also tell her that you think it's time for you to quit ballet class.

"I'll never be able to dance like you," you say sadly.

Neely's face falls. She's silent for a moment, and then she says, "But why be like me? If you try so hard to be like me, who is going to be like *you*?"

The question confuses you at first, but then you kind of get it. And you know that Neely's right. It's time to start figuring out your own talents instead of trying to copy someone else's.

The thought gives you a little hope. As you leave the classroom for the last time, you feel huge relief, too. You step lightly along the path toward home, your feet doing a one-of-a-kind dance of their very own.

The End

You feel bad about Riley's quitting. Is it partly your fault? Maybe you should have spent more time with her in class and made her feel like she was part of a team.

You also feel a little bit angry. Riley is so *good* at ballet, and you're not. How can she throw it all away?

Neely is more understanding about Riley's decision than you are. "What a person is good at and what she loves doing aren't always the same thing," Neely explains to you.

That makes sense, you suppose, but it still seems unfair.

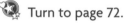 Turn to page 72.

> What a person is good at and what she loves doing aren't always the same thing.

After a sleepless night, you walk wearily to the Star Student Center for breakfast. You see Neely standing in line by herself—the perfect opportunity to tell her how you're feeling. You fall in line behind Neely, and after a little bit of chitchat, you finally ask her if it's okay for you to bow out of the show.

"I just don't think I'm ready," you say sadly. "Maybe next time."

Neely gives you that look that says *Don't be silly. You* are *ready.* But she's nice enough to say that you don't have to perform if you don't want to.

Neely thinks you're nervous, that you have cold feet. What you really have is a case of the "not-good-enoughs." You can't tell Neely that, though. You're too embarrassed, and you know she'll just say some nice (but not necessarily *true*) things to try to make you feel better. No, you'll just sit out this show—and hope that you'll feel better prepared for the next one.

In class that afternoon, everyone is chattering about the performance. You feel a little left out, but you remind yourself that you're still a part of the team. You'll focus on cheering on your friends. And when the show is over? You'll start looking for ways to encourage *yourself*, too.

The End

As you're leaving the locker room, your head hanging low, you run into Isabel. She's wearing a great costume—a fringed purple skirt and a top hat—and carrying a cane.

"Dress rehearsals for our tap routine," she explains to you. "Our costumes came in early."

Isabel is shining from head to toe, but she quickly sees that you're not. "What's wrong?" she asks.

You tell her, in as few words as possible, how you're feeling about ballet. "I stink," you say. "And Riley quit."

"I'm sorry," says Isabel. She gives you a sympathetic smile. Then she says, "Why don't you sit in on my class? You might like it better than ballet." Isabel does a tap step, and her fringed skirt shimmies. That makes you smile.

If you sit in on a tap class, turn to page 35.

If you stick with ballet, turn to page 82.

Dance Lessons

The next afternoon, you, Riley, and Shelby are doing homework at the student center. When you break for a snack, you work up the nerve to ask them if they ever dislike what they see in the mirror when they're dancing. Much to your surprise, every one of them says *yes*.

"Sometimes I don't look in the mirror at all," Riley confesses. "I just focus on how my body feels."

Shelby has some great advice, too. "Pretend the girl you see in the mirror is a good friend," she says. "You'd never say mean things to a friend, would you?"

No, you sure wouldn't. You decide to try Shelby's trick the next chance you get.

🌟 Turn to page 80.

Pretend the girl you see in the mirror is a good friend.

You leave Neely in the dance studio and follow the narrow, winding hall that leads toward the performance area. You peek through the door and see that the stage is dark, the seats before it empty. You push the door open and wander down the long aisle toward the stage. It's so quiet that you find yourself tiptoeing.

You climb the steps to the stage and stand there, peering out at the shadowy seats, imagining them full of people. A ray of light filters in through the slit in the stage curtain, landing like a spotlight on the floor. You hear faint music coming from a nearby classroom. It inspires you to slide off your shoes and do a little dance in your stocking feet.

It feels good to be moving freely, without mirrors or rules. Pretty soon your little dance turns into something much bigger. You leap through the air the way Neely did that first night you saw her onstage. You spin around and around until you get dizzy. You tumble to the floor, but you don't stop dancing.

You kick your legs in the air while you shimmy your shoulders. You roll onto your stomach and then your knees, and you jump back up onto your feet, exploding out of yourself like a cork from a bottle. You're dancing to your own music now, the music in your head, and you don't hear the footsteps coming down the aisle toward you.

Turn to page 76.

"Wow!" says a voice from out of the darkness. You whirl around, and there's Neely, plunked down in a front-row seat. Her eyes are wide and so is her smile. She starts clapping enthusiastically. "That was really good!" she says.

You blush. You're humiliated from your head to your toes, which have now come to a dead stop onstage.

"I'm serious!" says Neely. "That was the best improv I've seen in a long time." When she sees the confusion on your face, Neely explains that *improvisation* means making up dance moves on the spot. "I did a lot of improvisation in a modern dance class here at U-Shine Hall," she says.

"I've never heard of that class," you confess.

"Really?" says Neely. "I think you'd love it. Modern dance is all about expressing your feelings. It's like talking with your body, kind of like what you were doing onstage."

You blush again. "Yeah, I guess I had a lot to say," you reply sheepishly.

Since you're already embarrassed, you decide to take this opportunity to tell Neely that you want to quit ballet. She understands your reasons. And she's thrilled when you say that maybe you *would* like to learn more about modern dance.

 Turn to page 88.

By show day, you feel ready—and very glad you stuck with ballet. All the dancers are buzzing around backstage. Your dance instructor and Nadia, the stage manager, are trying to make sure everything is in order.

Nadia broke her leg and is on crutches, which makes it hard for her to navigate around the piles of costumes and stage props. Instead, she calls out orders to the lighting and sound technicians over a headset. Her tone scares you at first, but then you see the twinkle in her eye, and you can see that she's having fun with all this, too.

Isabel is helping the dancers get ready in the dressing area. She did her own hair and makeup first, and she looks amazing. You almost wish you could be in the audience instead of backstage so that you could cheer her on during her tap performance.

When Nadia says that your routine is up next, your stomach starts doing major flip-flops. If you don't get a handle on your nerves, you might mess up onstage. You look around for someone to talk to.

 If you go find Riley, turn to page 81.

 If you talk to Nadia, turn to page 83.

That night, back in your room at Brightstar House, you step into your walk-in closet and stand in front of your full-length mirror. It's hard to look in the mirror and pretend that you're someone else. But if you squint your eyes and fire up your imagination, you can almost see Shelby's face in the mirror instead of your own.

You try it again in the dance studio the next afternoon. You imagine that your reflection is Shelby's, and you pretend that she's the one who is just learning ballet. You can tell that she's working really hard. She may not be as graceful as Neely, but she looks pretty good—there are lots of things you could compliment her on.

Nice, rounded arms, you tell yourself. *Your hands look great, too—good job relaxing your fingers.*

You find yourself smiling at "Shelby." Riley catches you grinning at your own reflection, and she waves playfully at you in the mirror. You giggle and blush. *Thank goodness for good friends*, you think. You make a promise that from now on, you're going to be a better friend to *yourself*.

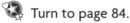 Turn to page 84.

You find Riley, who is fluffing up the skirt of her own shooting-star costume.

"Wow, you look nervous," she says after a quick glance at your face.

"Thanks," you say sarcastically. "That's really helpful."

Riley laughs. "I'm sorry," she says. "I guess it wasn't. Do you want to try one of the breathing tricks I use to help with nerves before soccer games?"

"Definitely," you say. You're willing to try anything at this point.

Riley shows you how to take a deep breath, hold it for a count of three, and then let it go. After a few deep breaths, you do start to feel a little calmer.

When it's time to line up in the wings, Riley gives you one more piece of advice. "If you forget the routine," she says, "just follow the dancer in front of you." She winks and wishes you luck. Then the curtains open, and you're on.

Turn to page 96.

"Thanks," you tell Isabel. "But I'd better stick with ballet, at least until the recital."

Isabel's eyes brighten at the word *recital*. "Ooh, you'll be getting your costume soon, too," she says. "Wearing a glittery new costume always makes me dance better. Maybe it'll work for you, too!"

"Maybe," you say. "But that still seems like a long way away." You sigh.

Isabel looks thoughtful. "Why wait that long?" she says. "I know how we can put some sparkle in your step *today*."

You're not sure what Isabel is up to, but you agree to meet her back at Brightstar House after dinner. When she shows up at your door, she's carrying a small white box wrapped with a pink polka-dot bow. Isabel is so excited that she can barely contain herself. "Open it!" she urges.

You slide off the bow and open the lid of the box. There, wrapped carefully in shiny tissue paper, is a new pair of satin ballet slippers. You're speechless.

"They're much more elegant than leather shoes, don't you think?" asks Isabel.

You do. You reach out to give Isabel a hug, but she ducks away. "Wait, there's more!" she says with a smile.

Beneath the slippers is a silver headband wrapped with pink ribbon. You're pretty sure Isabel made it herself. When you put it on, you feel as if you're wearing a tiara.

Turn to page 86.

Nadia is busy, but not too busy to take a moment to talk with you and help you calm your nerves.

"I'm always nervous before a performance, too," she says sweetly.

Nadia's words surprise you. "I didn't know you were a dancer!" you say.

"I am," Nadia replies. "And it's really hard to sit out the season with a broken leg. Believe me, I'd much rather be out there onstage than back here, watching from the wings."

You can see the sadness in Nadia's eyes, and that makes you determined not to let a silly thing like stage-fright get in the way of your own dancing. Talking with Nadia helps you put things in perspective. You decide that you'll dance your best tonight, for Nadia—who can't.

Turn to page 91.

When Neely announces that your class is going to have a routine in the next dance recital, you're thrilled! You've been much more patient and kind with yourself lately. You actually kind of like what you're seeing in the mirror now—a girl who is slowly but surely becoming a ballerina.

As performance day draws near, you and Riley practice extra hard. You'll play the parts of shooting stars dressed in sparkly silver tutus. You rehearse in front of Shelby, Isabel, and your stuffed animals—a pretend audience.

Dancing in front of your friends makes you feel more confident. They're so encouraging, and they help you have *fun* while you dance instead of taking it all so seriously. You wish there was a way that all of your friends could be with you on performance day. Hmm . . . *Is* there a way?

 If you invite your friends to be backstage with you before the show, turn to page 92.

 If you look for a way to actually dance with your friends on show day, turn to page 87.

Isabel is right: your new satin slippers and headband *do* help you dance better during your next ballet class. You stand a little taller, move a little more gracefully, and smile every time you look in the mirror.

Neely compliments you at the end of class. "You seemed so happy today while you were dancing," she says. "You looked great!"

You smile, grateful to Neely for noticing. You're about to show her your secret weapon—your new shoes. But as you slide out of your slippers, you see that the pink satin already looks dirty. The toe of one of the slippers is even a little bit scuffed.

You can't believe you've ruined them already. In that moment, you feel as if you've ruined *everything*. You can't hold it in anymore. Your tears start to flow, right there in front of Neely.

If you hurry out of class, turn to page 90.

If you let Neely comfort you, turn to page 101.

You knock on Neely's bedroom door at Brightstar House. You can hear her inside, practicing the saxophone. When she answers the door, you barely recognize her—her brown hair is spilling down over her shoulders rather than tucked up in a tidy dancer's bun.

"Hey!" Neely says. "What's up?"

You get right to the point. You ask Neely if there's any way that Shelby and Isabel can have really small parts in the ballet routine. "They've been great practice partners," you say, "and they're good dancers."

Neely thinks about it for a moment, which makes you hopeful. Then she says, "It's probably too late for that. But maybe you can all put on a short routine of your own during intermission. Would you be up for that?"

"Yes!" you say without hesitating. "What a great idea!"

When your dance instructor gives you the green light, you're doubly excited. And then the panic settles in. So far, you and your friends have just been playing around with dance steps. You haven't put them together into any kind of routine. Where will you start?

Turn to page 95.

You decide to sit in on a modern dance class, and Neely joins you for moral support. There's no sitting on the sidelines in this class, though. As soon as the lesson begins, the instructor invites you and Neely to stand up and take part in the warm-up.

The warm-up sounds a little confusing at first. You're supposed to try to smile and then frown using your *entire* body. You're surprised to find, though, that the smile is easy for you. You throw your arms over your head and wiggle your body from your head to your toes.

The frown is tougher to act out, maybe because you're having too much fun to act sad. Plus, Neely's "body frown" is hilarious. She slumps her shoulders and lets her arms hang loose. She gives them a little shake, and they flop from side to side. You have to look away to avoid falling into a heap of giggles.

After watching the first modern dance class, you don't have to think twice about signing up—this class just feels *right*. You talk with the instructor after class, and she invites you to join right away.

Neely's thrilled. "This means I'll still be seeing you all the time," she chatters excitedly. "Your classroom is right down the hall from mine. And we can hang out backstage during the next recital. And we—"

"Whoa," you interrupt her. "Recital? There's no way I'll be ready for the modern dance routine in the recital. That's just a few weeks away!"

"Are you sure?" Neely asks. "You *might* be ready."

There's no way, you think again to yourself. But a part of you wonders.

During the next lesson, you ask your modern dance instructor about the recital. You're surprised when she says that the choice is up to you. Do you want to work hard to catch up in time for the show, or do you want to sit out the first show and take part in the next?

 If you decide to sit out the first performance, turn to page 94.

If you decide to perform with the modern dance class, turn to page 98.

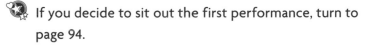

You hide in the locker room, feeling as worn out and frayed as the tips of your new shoes. You've tried to stick with ballet, but you don't have the energy to keep doing it.

You run your fingers over the smooth satin of your shoes. As your tears dry, you realize that the shoes aren't *that* dirty. Maybe you can clean them up and give them to someone else, a girl who will have more fun wearing them.

Maybe after that, you can figure out what's fun for *you*—what you love to do. Your passion must be out there somewhere, but you won't find it in this locker room. You gather your things, close your locker, and walk toward the door.

The End

Your routine starts out strong. You've never felt more graceful or more confident, and you don't have to remind yourself to smile—it's easy when you're feeling this good. Everything goes perfectly, as if the stars are aligned in the sky above you.

And then the music . . . suddenly . . . *stops*.

You freeze—everything seems to freeze. It's so quiet, you could hear a pin drop. You glance backstage and see Nadia talking frantically with one of the technicians. When she sees you looking her way, she raises her hands, palms up, as if to say, *I don't know what happened!* Her hands are poised and elegant, like a dancer's. And that gives you an idea.

 Turn to page 105.

Isabel and Shelby agree to hang out backstage with you and Riley on show day. Isabel gets dressed for her part in the tap-dance routine, and then she offers to do your hair and makeup.

"Do you want a classic ballet bun like Neely's?" she asks, looking at your reflection in the mirror.

You think about that for a moment and then shake your head. "Give me a special twist," you say. "Something that's more me."

Isabel grins and says she has just the thing. She puts three tiny braids in the front of your hair before gathering it all into a bun in back.

Shelby helps, too. She warms up Riley and you with a fun jazz routine. It reminds you of all the hours you spent dancing and laughing with your friends, and that thought relaxes you.

When the stage manager calls you into the wings to line up, you feel ready. Shelby gives you a hug for good luck, and then she hurries out to find her seat in the audience. As you listen to the muffled applause coming from beyond the curtain, you close your eyes and try to hang on to the good feeling you have right now. You stay in that warm, happy place until Riley nudges you.

"This is it," she whispers. You take a deep breath and then follow the other dancers onto the stage.

Turn to page 107.

You decide to sit out the first show, just to be sure that you're really ready before you take the stage.

On the big day, you sit in the audience watching your modern dance classmates perform, which is so exciting. You're looking forward to the time when you can be up there with them.

Next up in the show is a ballet performance, and your heart leaps when you see Neely step onto the stage. Her dancing still takes your breath away, but it's different this time. Instead of wishing you were her, you're just proud and happy for her. And you imagine the day when you'll be standing in the wings beside Neely, waiting for your *own* dance to begin.

The End

Luckily, when you share the news about the routine with your dance buddies, they have some ideas.

"I just downloaded the latest Strawberries video," Riley says. "They have some cool moves we could put in our routine."

"Good idea!" you say. The Strawberries are a great band, and they *do* know how to dance.

"Or how about this?" says Isabel, who's already off and running with her own idea. "We could invite a bunch of friends over for a dance party Friday night. I bet we could come up with a whole routine just by watching each other. How fun would that be?"

Pretty fun, you think, nodding enthusiastically. You're starting to feel a little less panicky about this routine—and a lot more excited. Which idea do you vote for?

⭐ If you vote for having a dance party, turn to page 102.

⭐ If you vote for trying some of the Strawberries' dance moves, go online to innerstarU.com/secret and enter this code: BREALBU

Once you're onstage, there's no time to be nervous. The music starts, and your body begins to dance as if on its own. You focus on your form and remind yourself to smile.

You're still nervous, but you feel better now that you're actually dancing. This is the moment when all of your hard work is paying off. Your confidence grows with each step you take—until the music suddenly *stops*.

The silence is deafening. You glance backstage and see the stage crew scrambling. Nadia is talking into her headset and motioning to a technician. She looks terrified.

You look around at the other dancers. They're frozen, and they're all looking at *you*, because the music ended when you were in the front row!

You can't hide behind anyone. You can't follow the dancer in front of you. And although you can't see the audience through the stage lights, you're sure that they're all staring at you, too, waiting for you to do something— *anything*.

If you panic and run from the stage, turn to page 99.

If you stay onstage, turn to page 100.

You make the bold decision to take part in the show, but you don't stop there. You make an even bolder decision to do a modern dance solo. Neely convinces you that making up a routine of your own might be easier than trying to catch up with the other dancers and learn their moves. You like that idea, but now you have to come up with a dance.

"Think of something that inspires you," Neely suggests.

What inspires me? you think. That's easy—Neely does, and all of your friends at Innerstar U. Each one of them has different talents and interests.

You decide to make up a dance that includes a little bit of each friend: a few ballet moves for Neely, some tap-dance moves for Isabel, and even a yoga-inspired move for Riley.

 Turn to page 104.

The next ten seconds feel like ten hours. The lights above you sear into your skin, and you feel sweat pool in your ballet slippers. When you can't take it anymore, you fall out of line and run swiftly from the stage. You don't know what else to do—you just want to get out of the spotlight.

Of course, the moment you get backstage, the music starts up again. Nadia calls to the dancers to pick up where they left off, but they can't seem to pull it together. They're short a shooting star, and that messes up the lineup. You're too embarrassed to go back out there and join them.

You hide backstage, humiliated. Someone puts her hand on your shoulder. It's Neely. You're afraid she's going to be upset with you, but instead, she just feels bad for you—and a little guilty about talking you into staying in ballet, now that you've had such a horrible experience.

It's a funny thing: seeing Neely look so blue actually makes you feel less upset. "It's okay," you say to Neely, and as the words come out of your mouth, you know they're true. You've worked really hard these last few weeks, and you've learned a lot.

"For what it's worth," Neely says, "you looked great out there—I mean, until the music stopped." She smiles, and you can't help smiling, too. With Neely beside you, you'll be able to face the other dancers after the show. And maybe—just maybe—you'll be able to set foot onstage again someday, too.

The End

As the silence drags on, you try not to panic. *You're a shooting star,* you remind yourself. *What would a shooting star do?*

Then it comes to you. You start with a star jump, a burst of sparkle and shine. Then you skip swiftly and softly across the stage like a star streaking through the night sky. In the midst of your solo star dance, you hear footsteps behind you. You glance backward and are surprised to see that Riley is following you, a huge smile on her face. Her arms are spinning and streaking through the "sky." And then, from behind her, another star steps from her place to follow, and then another.

You're flying high now. You do a series of *chaine* turns, swirling your arms overhead. But you have to remind yourself that shooting stars don't last long. You twirl more slowly now, and slower still. Then you let yourself fall, gracefully, to the stage.

One by one, the dancers behind you fall, too, until the last dancer rests. The audience bursts into applause.

Turn to page 108.

When Neely realizes you're upset about your shoes, she smothers a giggle of relief. "Take a look at these," she says.

Neely pulls her own pointe shoes out of her ballet bag. You nearly giggle, too, when you see just how dirty and worn Neely's shoes are. You give her a grateful smile.

Of course, the real reason you're upset has nothing to do with shoes. It's time to tell Neely the truth—that ballet just isn't for you.

"It's okay," Neely says. "I love ballet, but that doesn't mean you have to. Figure out what *you* love to do, and then do it!" It sounds so simple when she puts it that way.

Turn to page 110.

Figure out what you love to do, and then do it!

You all pitch in to help Isabel throw a dance party. You rearrange her furniture to make space for a dance floor and you set a disco ball on a table in the middle of the room. The ball spins in circles, sending colored light dancing across the walls.

As music fills the room, your friends pull out their funkiest dance moves. You do, too. You close your eyes and give it everything you've got, shaking and shimmying your body. You're lost in your own little world.

When a song ends and there's sudden silence, you open your eyes. You're shocked to see that some of your friends are watching you, wide-eyed and giggling.

 If you hurry off the dance floor, turn to page 112.

 If you crack a joke about your dancing, turn to page 115.

It's as if your friends know that you're performing a dance of friendship, because they all turn out for your big day. Isabel helps you with your hair and makeup backstage. And when you peek out at the audience before the lights go down, you see your other friends in the front row.

That makes you nervous at first, but when you actually take the stage, you can't see the faces in the crowd—the stage lights blind you. That's good, because in the darkness, you remember to dance for *yourself* rather than to worry about others. Your performance goes off without a hitch, and it feels so good!

Afterward, Neely presents you with a beautiful bouquet of flowers. Most of the dancers get roses, but your flowers are unique and exotic. "They're one of a kind," says Neely, "just like you."

The End

You feel your own hands lift slowly and elegantly from your sides. You remember the *port de bras*, the arm movements you practiced over and over again in class. You find your arms working through them one by one.

Your arms move swiftly at first—like a shooting star burning brightly as it falls through the sky. You let yourself fall slowly and gracefully to the stage.

You're sitting now, with one leg crossed in front of the other, but your arms are still dancing. They weave through the air as you lower your chest toward your knees. When your forehead touches the floor, your arms wind downward, ever so slowly, and come to a rest on the stage in front of you.

There's a moment of silence, and then the audience starts clapping and cheering.

Turn to page 106.

While the audience applauds, Nadia calls you and the other dancers offstage.

"That was so *brave*," she says to you, her voice thick with admiration. "What inspired your 'arm ballet'?"

"That's easy," you say, grinning. "*You* did, with your graceful hands—and with your grace under pressure."

Nadia seems pleased about that, and also a little embarrassed.

"Who knew you could dance with nothing but your arms?" Riley says, giving you a high five.

Neely rushes over, too, to compliment you on your choreography. "You can help me create a dance routine any day," she says to you.

Neely's comment plants a seed in your mind, an idea for a dance you could create that is made up of nothing but arm movements. Now you know that you have to stick with another season of ballet. There's someone else here who you hope might come back to class soon, too.

You smile at Nadia, your new friend, and she waves back—the graceful wave of a dancer.

The End

The stage lights are blinding. You scan the dark crowd looking for Shelby, but you can't make out her face. Your heart pounds in your ears.

When the music starts, you abandon your search and struggle to remember your first steps. Luckily, Riley's standing in front of you. You follow her moves, and pretty soon you fall into the routine that you've worked so hard to learn. You *chassé* across the stage, taking graceful sideways steps.

All's well until it's time for you and the other dancers in your row to step to the front. You're nervous about being so close to the audience. What if you don't look as elegant as the dancers beside you?

As you take an awkward step toward the crowd, your foot suddenly slips. Your leg slides out from beneath you and you land, with a harsh *thud*, on the stage.

In that moment, everything seems to stop—the music, the dancers, your heart in your chest. You imagine that any moment now, the crowd is going to burst out laughing.

 If you get up and hurry off the stage, turn to page 109.

 If you get up and keep dancing, turn to page 111.

When you and the other dancers are backstage again, everyone gathers around you to congratulate you on your quick thinking. You get huge kudos from Neely, from your instructor, and even from Nadia, the stage manager—who says that you're a real lifesaver.

"You're also a master at improvisation," says Neely. "You know how to make up dance moves on the spot. That was amazing!"

"Thanks," you say. "I've never heard that word before. Improv—what?"

"*Improvisation*," says Neely again. "You'd hear the word a lot if you ever took a modern dance class. You should try one out. You'd be great at it!"

"I'll think about it," you say with a smile.

You appreciate the compliment. Right now, though, you're feeling pretty good about ballet. Tonight was your first performance, and you were a true shining star.

The End

You jump to your feet, your face and ears burning. There's no way you can keep dancing now. You just need to get out of here.

As you dash through the row of dancers behind you, you brush elbows with Riley, knocking her off balance. You mumble a quick apology as you run for the darkness and safety of the wings.

Nadia, the stage manager, tries to catch you as you hurry past. When she sees your face, though, she gives you a sympathetic smile and lets you go. She doesn't have time to comfort you right now. She has to make sure that nothing else goes wrong with the music, lights, or dancers onstage. *Why bother?* you think. You've already ruined the performance.

You hide in the shadows backstage until the routine is over. As the music ends, the dancers start spilling into the backstage area. They're smiling, their faces flushed—all except for Riley. You catch her eye and are surprised to see that she looks a little angry. She walks right past you and sits in the far corner of the backstage area, where she starts taking off her shoes.

You approach her slowly, not sure what's wrong. "Riley?" you say softly. But she won't look at you.

Turn to page 114.

Another dancer has a question for Neely. When Neely steps away, you pick up her pointe shoes. They're still beautiful, even all scuffed up. You remember how Neely looked wearing them during her last performance. You remember how much you wished that it was you up there, dancing gracefully onstage.

You slide your foot into one of Neely's pointe shoes. The shoe is hard and tight—it pinches your foot. You quickly pull it off and set it down.

"Doesn't fit?" Neely asks, grinning, as she comes up from behind you. You shake your head, a little embarrassed that she caught you.

Neely giggles. "I've worn them enough that they've molded to my feet," she explains. "Now they fit my feet perfectly—no one else's. Kind of like Cinderella's glass slippers."

That makes you laugh out loud, which feels good. As you leave the studio with Neely, you remind yourself that ballet dancing is her dream, not yours. You'll have to keep searching to figure out what *you* love—and find your own fairy-tale ending.

The End

In that moment, when you're sprawled very *ungracefully* onstage, you scan the crowd again for Shelby. You need to see a friendly face right now. You can't see her, but you know she's out there somewhere.

You picture Shelby's face in your mind. She's smiling at you. *Get up, goofball*, she says. *Get up and keep dancing.*

You jump to your feet and imagine that you're in your room at Brightstar House. You pretend that the audience in the shadows is Shelby, Isabel, and your favorite stuffed animals. The thought relaxes you.

You do a quick curtsy for your friends to tell them that you're okay. There's a ripple of laughter from the audience, and then some applause. Are they clapping for you? You smile and fall back in line, ready to keep dancing.

 Turn to page 116.

You make up some excuse about being thirsty, and you head to the snack table to get a drink. You wish you could crawl *under* the table. You were just having fun and trying some new moves, but it's obvious from the looks on your friends' faces that you should stick with ballet. At least in ballet, it's clear where your feet and arms should be at all times.

You pour a cup of punch and then busy yourself with chips and dip. When a Strawberries song comes on, Riley calls you to the dance floor, but you take a pass. You've just spotted the brownies—your favorite comfort food.

You're well into your third brownie when Isabel comes up from behind you and tugs at your arm. "Come *on*," she says. "You're missing all the fun!"

You shake your head. "My dashing shinks," you say.

"Huh?" she asks.

You swallow the last of your brownie and say, "I said my dancing stinks."

When performance day comes, you're more than ready. Your ballet routine is first, and you and Riley shine as shooting stars. You feel polished, poised, and in control. You're the picture of elegance—at least in your own mind!

At intermission, you and your friends hit the stage for a different kind of dance: one full of fun, energetic moves that get the crowd clapping and cheering. You're in the middle of the routine when you catch sight of Shelby beside you. She's doing the silly shoulder shrugs, the same ones that you taught her at Isabel's party. Shelby grins at you and shrugs her shoulders all the way up to her ears. You burst out laughing. You can't remember the last time you had so much fun.

By the end of the performance, you feel like a real dancer. You're determined to keep doing what you've been doing, because it's working. You need to keep challenging yourself and learning new techniques through ballet. You also need to bust out sometimes and make up your own moves with friends. The more you dance, the better you'll get—and the more fun you'll have, too!

The End

It's hard for you to remember the moves you just did, so you make up some new, equally funky moves. Shelby grabs her camera and records you. She plays the clip back, and you can't help giggling. It's not that you're a bad dancer. You just look like you're having so much fun!

The recording helps you feel better about your dancing, and it helps you and your friends plan your routine, too. You take turns recording one another dancing, and then you play back the clips so that you can teach each other your favorite moves. Later that night, you put them all together into a fun routine.

Minutes later, as Neely steps onto the stage, you can't help admiring her grace and her form. *She's the real dancer,* you think to yourself. But you've learned a lot from her— and from your other friends. You're well on your way.

The End

> Everyone makes mistakes, but a real dancer picks herself up and keeps going.

In what feels like just seconds later, the show is over. You made it through! You curtsy for the second time tonight and then you follow Riley and the other dancers off the stage.

Neely greets you in the wings and gives you a huge hug. Riley throws her arms around you, too. Not long after that, Shelby and Isabel squeeze their way into the group to congratulate you.

"You did *great*," Shelby says.

"Did you like my solo?" you joke.

"That was the best part," Isabel says. "Your curtsy, and that big smile on your face afterward. That made the whole performance more fun."

"Isabel's right," Neely agrees. "Everyone makes mistakes, but a real dancer picks herself up and keeps on going."

"Well, I did have help," you say. "All I could hear was Shelby's voice in my head saying, 'Get up! Get going!'"

Shelby's jaw drops. She grins and then punches your shoulder playfully.

"Speaking of," says Riley to Neely, "isn't it time for *you* to get going?"

Neely's eyes widen. Her solo routine is next, and she totally lost track of time. But another team of dancers has taken the stage, and there are still a couple of minutes left in their routine. Neely breathes a sigh of relief and then leans against the wall to do some stretching. You give her a quick hug for good luck.

You take a bow in the middle of Isabel's makeshift dance floor. "Show's over," you say, trying to make your voice sound light. "I promise to stop dancing if you'll stop laughing."

Shelby sees the wounded look in your eyes, and she throws her arm around you. "Don't stop," she says quickly. "That was some crazy dancing, but you made up lots of great moves! I want to try that shoulder thing you do."

"And the hip thing," says Riley. "How'd you do that?"

It takes you a minute to realize that your friends are serious. They actually want you to teach them some of the moves that you pulled out of thin air.

 Turn to page 118.

You can't figure out why Riley is upset with you. After all, you're the one who fell and made a fool of yourself. But then Neely, who saw the whole performance, pulls you aside.

"Riley fell, too," she explains, "after you ran into her onstage. She got up and kept going, but it was a rough performance for her. She made lots of mistakes."

Oh, no! You feel terrible. "I just had to get out of there after screwing up," you say sadly.

Neely puts her arm around you. "I understand," she says. "I've been there. But the first rule of performing is that if you make a mistake, keep going. Chances are, no one will remember your mistake. But if you stop, they will."

You sigh. Neely's right. You won't ever forget what happened today, and Riley probably won't either. You were so worried about your mistake that you abandoned your team—and your favorite teammate.

Rule number two, you think to yourself—*if you want your friends to be there for you, remember to be there for them.* You take a deep breath and start walking toward Riley. You have some apologizing to do.

The End

Isabel gives you a stern look. "Your dancing *doesn't* stink," she says. "I really admire that you aren't afraid to try new moves."

You snort and drop your gaze. "I guess some of them work better than others," you mumble, flicking a crumb off your sleeve.

"Maybe," says Isabel. "But the ones that work are *really* cool, and we need more of those in our dance routine." She sounds pretty sincere. You want to believe her.

"C'mon . . ." Isabel coaxes. "We need you!"

You finally agree to step back onto the dance floor. The more you think about Isabel's words, the more sense they make. If you and your friends have any hope of coming up with a whole new dance routine, you're going to have to get creative. And being creative takes courage.

What definitely *doesn't* help creativity is a stomach-ache. Maybe you had one brownie too many. You leave the party early, after promising your friends that you'll meet up with them again tomorrow. And when you do, you'll bring your creativity, along with the courage you need to express it.

The End